I LIKE TO EAT CHILDREN

a children's horror story by

REAGAN ROTHE

Illustrated by Drew Rose

PUBLISHED BY BLACK ROSE WRITING

www.blackrosewriting.com

Printed in the United States of America

For Lena Louise,
The precious little star that even the
scariest of creatures couldn't dare scare!

For Walter Lee,
The fiercest little Mandalorian that
creates infinite happy chaos!

There is a creature lurking.

It began in your nightmares.

But now, it's real.

It has no name.

It has already eaten all the goblins
and witches and mummies
and zombies and ghouls.

But unlucky for you...

It likes to eat children!

It has dark green skin, scaly and slimy and full of oozing yellow bumps.

It has one large eye in the middle of its forehead.

The creature's eye glows a bright red, especially when searching for children.

It has six sharp fangs in its foaming mouth.

And six sharp claws on its spiny fingers.

And did I mention, **It likes to eat children!**

It has wart-covered ears, for listening.

And a big nose, for smelling.

It has webbed feet, for swimming.

And spiraled horns, for stabbing.

It has a large belly, for feeding.

And it has no heart... no heart at all, for
feeling no pity, nor grief,
nor remorse.

Beware little kids, **It likes to eat children!**

Mae and Myer look under their beds.

Nothing but scattered toys and boxes.

Max searches her closet.

Nothing but stuffed animals and hanging clothes.

Wyatt and Maggie turn on their color-changing lamps.

The light shows nothing in the room, no monsters,
no noises, no signs of any scary things at all.

Only a bad dream, but still, **It likes to eat children!**

7

And when darkness arrives, and the sun has left.

Shapes begin to change and take on an eerie form.

But don't always believe your eyes, no matter one or two.

The mind plays tricks, it's not always true.

The creature that eats children isn't real.

Or is it?

"I've come for you!
I like to eat children!

Run and hide as fast as you can.

It chases after you.

And it comes closer...

And closer...

And closer...

And then it's sharp claws reach for the back of your neck,
and it's sharp fangs are behind you.

Run faster! **It likes to eat children!**

But then mom and dad come to your rescue,
just in the nick of time.

They stand front and center,
waving a finger in the creature's spooky face.

The creature is now the one that is scared.

And it says, "I'm sorry, I will leave now."

You smile as it goes,
knowing your parents are the real heroes.

After all,
It likes to eat children!
but not grownups!

In loving memory of Max Reagan Rothe Simmons

Reagan Rothe not only writes books, but he publishes them as well. *I Like to Eat Children* is his second children's story and sixth published book overall.

He currently resides with his beautiful and amazing wife, Minna, and his precious daughter, Lena, in Castroville, TX. Rothe spends much of his non-writing time mountain biking and watching sports.

BLACK ROSE writing™

Made in the USA
Coppell, TX
08 August 2021

60158343R00017

Have you crossed paths with the creature who likes to eat children? If your answer is no, then you are one lucky kid.

Because there is a creature lurking. It began in your nightmares. But now, it's real. It has no name.

And it likes to eat children!

ISBN 979-8-5898-3221-1

51295

9 798589 832211

T4-AZS-449

BLACK ROSE writing™

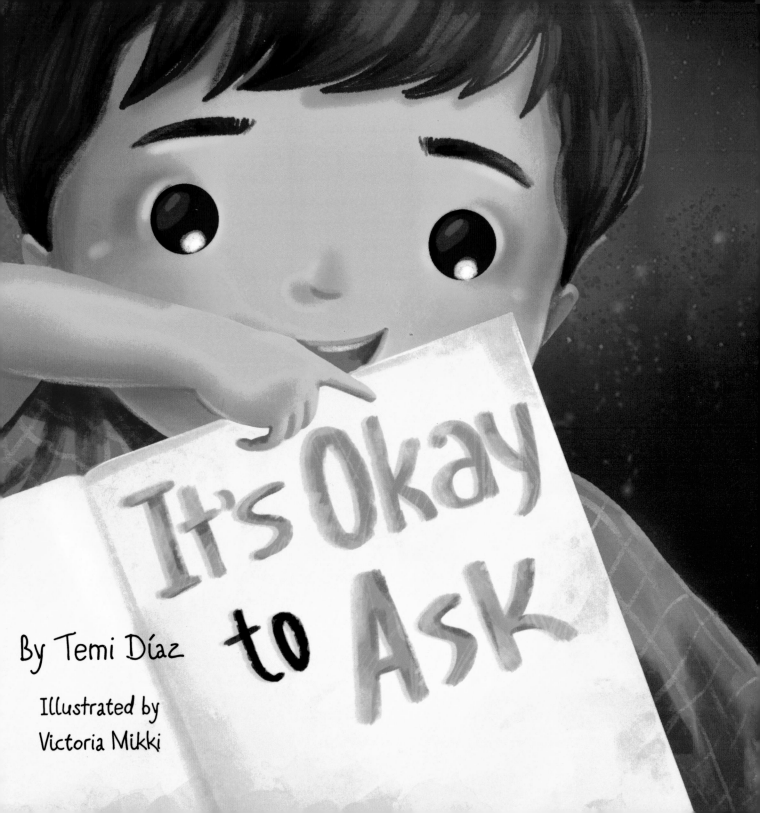

By Temi Díaz

Illustrated by
Victoria Mikki